MW00423035

PENGUIN
SPECIALS

Penguin Specials fill a gap. Written by some of today's most exciting and insightful writers, they are short enough to be read in a single sitting – when you're stuck on a train; in your lunch hour; between dinner and bedtime. Specials can provide a thought-provoking opinion, a primer to bring you up to date, or a striking piece of fiction. They are concise, original and affordable.

To browse digital and print Penguin Specials titles, please refer to **www.penguin.com.au/penguinspecials**

ALSO BY MO YAN

Radish

MO YAN

Translated from the original
Chinese by Howard Goldblatt

PENGUIN BOOKS

UK | USA | Canada | Ireland | Australia
India | New Zealand | South Africa | China

Penguin Books is part of the Penguin Random House group of companies
whose addresses can be found at global.penguinrandomhouse.com

Penguin
Random House
PENGUIN BOOKS CHINA

This paperback edition published by Penguin Group (Australia)
in association with Penguin (Beijing) Ltd, 2016

3 5 7 9 10 8 6 4 2

Text copyright © Mo Yan, 2015

Translated from the Chinese by Howard Goldblatt

Originally published in Chinese as 'Tou Ming De Hong Luo Bo'
by *Chinese Writers Magazine*, 1985

The moral right of the author has been asserted.

All rights reserved. Without limiting the rights under copyright reserved above, no part
of this publication may be reproduced, stored in or introduced into a retrieval system,
or transmitted, in any form or by any means (electronic, mechanical, photocopying,
recording or otherwise), without the prior written permission of both the copyright
owner and the above publisher of this book.

Cover design by Di Suo © Penguin Group (China)
Text design by Steffan Leyshon-Jones © Penguin Group (China)
Printed and bound in Hong Kong by Printing Express

ISBN: 9780734310798

penguin.com.cn

MIX
Paper from
responsible sources
FSC™ C012285

Chapter One

An autumn morning, the air thickly humid, a layer of transparent dewdrops clung to blades of grass and roof tiles. Leaves on the scholar tree had begun to turn yellow; a rusty iron bell hanging from a branch was also dew laden. The production team leader, a padded jacket draped over his shoulders, ambled toward the bell, carrying a sorghum flatbread in one hand and clutching a thick-peeled leek in the other. By the time he reached the bell, his hands were empty, but his cheeks were puffed out like a field mouse scurrying away with autumn provisions. He yanked the clapper against the side of the bell, which rang out loudly – *clang, clang, clang*. People young and old streamed out of the lanes to converge beneath the bell, eyes fixed on the team leader, like a crowd of marionettes. He swallowed hard, and wiped his stubble-ringed mouth on his sleeve. All eyes watched that mouth as it opened – to spit out a stream of curses: 'I'll be fucked if those stupid commune pricks aren't taking two of our stonemasons one day and two carpenters the next. He turned to a tall, broad-shouldered young man. 'They're breaking up our workforce. The commune plans to widen the floodgate behind the village, mason,' he said to him. 'Every team has to send them a mason and an unskilled labourer. It might as well be you.'

The handsome young mason had black eyebrows and white teeth, the contrast lending him a heroic bearing. A gentle shake of his head sent back a lock of hair that had fallen over his forehead. Speaking with a slight stammer, he asked who the unskilled labourer would be.

The team leader folded his arms, as if to fight off the cold, and rolled his eyes like pinwheels. 'A woman makes the most sense,' he rasped, 'but we need them for picking cotton, and sending a man would be a waste of manpower.' He looked around and his gaze fell on the wall. A boy of ten or so stood in a corner. He was barefoot and stripped to the waist, wearing only a pair of long, baggy, green-striped white shorts that were stained by grass and dried blood. The shorts ended at his knees, above calves shiny with scars.

'I see you're still with us, Hei-hai, you little shit!' the team leader said as he studied the boy's jutting breast-bone. 'I thought you'd gone down to meet the King of Hell. Are you over the shakes?'

The boy didn't respond, just kept his bright black

eyes fixed on the team leader. He had a big head and a skinny neck that seemed in danger of snapping from the load it carried.

'Feel like earning a few work points? Though I don't know what a pitiful little thing like you could possibly do. A fart would knock you off your feet. Go with the mason to the floodgate, how's that? But first run home and get a hammer, then you can sit up there and smash rocks, as many as you feel like, or as few. If history's any judge, these commune jobs are just busy work meant to fool the foreign devils.'

The boy shuffled up to the mason and tugged at his jacket. He was rewarded with a friendly pat on his shaved gourd of a head. 'Go home and ask your stepmother for a hammer, and I'll meet you at the bridgehead.'

The boy took off. He had all the appearance of running, his rail-thin arms flailing like a scarecrow in the wind, but none of the speed. All eyes were on him, and as they looked at his bare back, they suddenly felt the cold. The team leader tugged at his jacket. 'When you get home,' he shouted, 'tell your stepmother to give you a shirt, you poor little beggar!'

He stole in quietly through the gate. A snot-nosed little boy with a pushed-in face was sitting in the yard, playing in the urine-wetted mud. He looked up and threw open his arms: 'Bro . . . bro . . . pick up . . .' Hei-hai bent down, picked up a light red apricot leaf to wipe his

3

stepbrother's nose, then slapped the snotty leaf onto the wall like a leaflet. He waved the boy off and slipped into the house, where he picked up a claw hammer from a corner and slipped back outside. The little boy called out again, so Hei-hai snatched up a fallen branch, drew a wide circle around his stepbrother on the ground, then tossed the branch away and sped to the rear of the village, where a medium-sized river flowed, spanned by a stone bridge with nine arched openings. Owing to summer floods, the trunks of weeping willows growing in profusion on the levee were covered with red fibrous roots. Now that the water had receded, the roots had dried out. The willow leaves had yellowed and fallen into the river, to be carried slowly downstream. Ducks gliding near the riverbank quacked as they dug their red beaks into aquatic grasses in search of food, though who knew if they found any.

The boy was wheezing by the time he reached the levee. His jutting breastbone seemed to contain a clucking hen.

'Hurry up, Hei-hai!' the mason shouted from the bridgehead.

Hei-hai, still appearing to be running, made his way over to the mason. 'Aren't you cold?' the mason asked as he looked him over.

Hei-hai just gaped at him. The mason was in work clothes – pants and jacket over a red athletic shirt, its

4

dazzling collar turned up flamboyantly. The boy stared at that collar as if it were a bonfire.

'What are you looking at?' the mason asked, rubbing the boy's head, which rocked back and forth like a drum rattle. 'You,' he said, 'your stepmother has knocked the sense right out of you.'

The mason whistled a tune, rapping his fingers on the boy's head as they walked onto the bridge. The boy stepped carefully to keep his head where the mason could rap it with thick knuckles that were hard as little clubs. It hurt, but he bore it silently, with only a slight wince. The mason could whistle just about anything with his moist, red lips. Puckering them up and spreading them a bit, he mimicked the crisp, melodic notes of a meadowlark and sent them soaring into the sky.

They crossed the bridge, climbed the levee and headed west to the floodgate, about half a *li* away. The floodgate was also a bridge of sorts, the difference being a flashboard that held back the water when it was down and released it when it was raised. The levee's gentle slope, densely covered with feathery river locusts, gave out onto a wide, spongy sandbank where wild grass was already taking root in the wake of the summer flood. Rich open country spread out beyond the levee as far as the eye could see, saturated from the annual floods with silt deposits that turned once hard black earth into fertile soil. The most recent flood had been light enough to spare the levee, so the gate had remained shut. The floodplain was so densely planted with Bengalese jute it was like a virgin forest. A light mist shrouded the field on that early morning, lending it an oceanic quality.

The mason and Hei-hai strolled up to the floodgate, where two teams waited on the sandy ground. Men made up one team, women the other, like a pair of rival camps. A commune cadre, notebook in hand, stood between the teams and gestured as he spoke to them, raising and lowering his arms. The mason led Hei-hai along the floodgate's concrete steps and walked up to the man. 'Reporting in from our village, Deputy Director Liu,' he said. He had often been temporarily assigned to the commune, where Director Liu was frequently in charge of projects, so they already knew each other.

Hei-hai was staring at Director Liu's broad mouth. When the purple lips that formed that mouth came together they produced a string of sounds: 'You again, you slippery devil. That damned village of yours sure knows how to meet quotas. They've sent me a man who could slip through the holes of any strainer. Just my luck. Where's your helper?'

Hei-hai felt the mason's knuckles on his head.

'Him?' Director Liu wrapped his hand around the boy's neck and wobbled his head back and forth. Hei-hai's heels nearly left the ground. 'Why send me this skinny little monkey?' he snarled. 'Can he even lift a hammer?'

'All right now, Director Liu Taiyang,' the mason said as he pried the man's hand from Hei-hai's neck. 'The glory of socialism is that everyone eats. Hei-hai comes from three generations of poor peasants. If socialism won't take care of him, who will? Besides, his mother's gone, and he lives with a stepmother. His daddy went off to the north-east like a man possessed and hasn't been home for three years. He might be bear food by now or lying in the bellies of wolves. Where's your class sentiment, Director Liu Taiyang?' This he said partly in jest.

Hei-hai was lightheaded from the shaking. He'd been close enough to the director to smell the alcohol on his breath, and it made him sick. It was what his stepmother smelled like much of the time. After his father left, she often sent him to the canteen to barter dried yams for alcohol, and she didn't stop drinking till she was drunk. That was when the beating and the pinching and the biting started.

'A skinny little monkey!' Director Liu spat out, then turned and continued lecturing the others.

Hammer in hand, Hei-hai scampered onto the floodgate, about a hundred metres long and a dozen or more metres tall, and fronted on the north by a rectangular trough, the same length as the floodgate itself. It contained the remnants of the summer floodwaters. The boy stood atop the floodgate, gripping the stone railing as he gazed down at the water, where scrawny black fish swam clumsily between the rocks. Both ends of the gate butted up against the towering levee, which was part of the road to the county town. There were stone railings, half a metre high, at each end of the five-metre-wide gate. A few years earlier, a passing horse cart had knocked a number of cyclists over the side, leading to broken legs and hips and even a fatality. He'd been younger then, of course, and had had a lot more meat on his bones. His father hadn't left for the north-east and his stepmother hadn't started drinking. He ran over to see what was going on, but arrived too late, after the cyclists had been taken away, and all that remained in the trough was muddy water stained red. His nose was keen enough to detect the stink of blood floating up from the water.

Gripping the cold white stone railing with one hand, he rapped it with his hammer, causing both railing and hammer to ring out. And as he listened intently to the sound, scenes from the past flitted in and out of his eyes before disappearing. A bright sun shone down on the jute field beyond the levee, and he watched a fine mist skitter among the plants. The fields were too densely planted: low to the ground there were gaps between the stalks, but the upper branches and leafy tops came together, damp and glistening. He let his eyes drift westward, past the jute field to a patch of sweet potatoes, where the fleshy purple leaves gleamed. Hei-hai knew they were a new variety, short vines heavily laden with potatoes bigger and sweeter than most, with white skins and red pulp; they burst open when cooked. A vegetable plot bordered the sweet potato patch to the north. Now that all private land had reverted to the commune, this is where production brigade members planted vegetables. Hei-hai knew that both the vegetable plot and the sweet potato patch belonged to a village five *li* away. It was one of the richer villages. The vegetable plot was planted with cabbages and radishes, whose long, lush tassels were such a deep green they were nearly black. A lonely two-room shed in the centre of the plot was home to a lonely old man. The boy knew all this. Jute plants as far as the eye could see spread out north of the field. The same was true to the west. With jute on three sides and the levee on the fourth, the sweet-potato plot and vegetable field looked like a big square well. As the boy's thoughts wandered, the purple and green leaves turned into autumn well water, and then the jute became water, while sparrows skimming the tips of the jute plants were transformed into green kingfishers snapping up tiny shrimp from the water's surface.

Deputy Director Liu was still lecturing. Here is what he said: If agriculture is to follow the Dazhai Commune model, irrigation will be its lifeblood. That's one of the points of the Eight Point Charter for Agriculture.

Agriculture without irrigation is like a child with no mother. Or a child with a mother with no breasts. Or it's a child with a mother with breasts but no milk. Without milk the child will die, or if it lives, it'll turn out like this little monkey (Director Liu pointed to Hei-hai, up on the floodgate. The boy had his back to the people and they could see two sun-illuminated scars streaking down his back like jagged lightning bolts). And besides, the gate is so narrow it claims lives every year. The commune's revolutionary committee takes this very seriously, and after studying the problem from all angles, we've decided to widen the gate. To get the job done, we've mobilised labourers from all brigades, more than two hundred of you. This is the first stage: girls and married women, young and old, plus the little monkey (he pointed a second time to Hei-hai up on the gate whose scars now shone like mirrors) will break up all the rocks within five hundred square metres to the size of restorative pills or egg yolks. Masons will then shape the pieces of stone appropriately. These are our two blacksmiths (he pointed to a pair of deeply-tanned men, one tall, the other short, one old, the other young), who will repair chisels the masons have dulled. Those of you who live close by will return to your villages for meals, the others will eat in the village up ahead, where we've set up a field kitchen. The same for sleeping: those who live farther away will spend the nights under the bridge openings (he pointed to the arched openings below the floodgate). The women will sleep from east to west, the men from west to east. Straw will be spread out on the ground for sleeping, fluffy as spring mattresses, too fucking comfy for the likes of you.

'Are you going to sleep under one, Director Liu?'

'I'm in charge, I've got a bicycle, and it's none of your business where I plan to sleep, so don't get your guts in a stew. Do soldiers ride horses just because their officer does? Now get your asses to work. You'll get plenty of work points, and I'll throw in a measure of water conservation grain and twenty water conservation cents. Anyone who doesn't want to work can fuck off. Even the little monkey will get money and rations, and by the time work on the gate is finished he'll have put on weight, you can bet on it.'

Hei-hai didn't hear a word Director Liu said. He had draped his skinny arms over the railing and was holding his hammer in both hands. He heard music like birdsong and the chirps of autumn insects from the jute field. The retreating mist seemed to thunder as it caromed off jute leaves and both deep red and light green stalks. The sound of grasshoppers rubbing legs against forewings was like a train crossing an iron bridge. He'd once seen a train in a dream, a one-eyed monster running at a crouch, faster than a horse. What if it had run standing up instead? The train had just stood up in his dream when he was awakened by a swat from his stepmother's hearth broom. She told him to fetch water from the river. The swat didn't hurt, that was just a blast of heat, but the sound was like someone far away clubbing a jute sack filled with cotton. With the carrying pole over his shoulder, he hooked on the full buckets of water; they barely cleared the ground, and he could hear his bones creak. His ribs pushed against his hipbones. Holding the swaying pole with both hands, he climbed the steep levee onto a path twisted by willow trees, whose trunks seemed fitted with magnets; they pulled the tinplate buckets away from him. One hit a tree and sloshed water onto the path, turning it so slippery it was like stepping on melon rinds. He fell awkwardly, and the water soaked him like a waterfall. His face smacked into the ground, flattening his nose, which was scored by a grassy stalk. Blood ran from his nose into his mouth. He spit out one mouthful, swallowed the next. His buckets sang merrily as they rolled down to the river. He clambered up and ran after them. One rested at an angle in riverbank reeds, the other was being carried downstream. He chased it down the riverbank, running on four-spined star thistle that he and the other kids called dog-turd grass. He tried to grip the burrs with his toes, but still slipped into the river. It was warm and nearly reached his navel. His shorts billowed out and wrapped around his waist like a jellyfish.

Now wading, he sloshed after his bucket, and when he caught it, he turned and headed back upstream, holding up the bucket in one hand and paddling with the other. The river ran hard, making him stumble as he leaned forward and thrust his neck out. It felt to him as if a school of tiny fish had encircled his legs, and began nibbling gently. He stopped, trying to capture the sensation, but it vanished. The river darkened, as if the fish were fleeing in panic. But the pleasant sensation returned once he started walking again. The fish were back, it seemed. This time he didn't stop, just kept forging ahead, eyes half shut, moving forward.

'Hei-hai!'

'Hei-hai!'

He snapped out of his reverie and opened his eyes. The fish vanished. The hammer slipped out of his hands and dropped into the green water below the gate, spraying a watery chrysanthemum into the air.

'That little monkey's not all there,' Director Liu said as he climbed onto the gate and grabbed the boy by the ear. 'Go on, go break rocks with the women and see if you can find a mother who'll take you in.'

The mason also came up onto the gate and rubbed the boy's cold scalp. 'Go on,' he said, 'go find your hammer. Break as much rock as you can. Then you can go play.'

'If I catch you loafing on the job, I'll cut your ear off

as a snack to go with my drink,' Director Liu thundered.

Hei-hai trembled. He slipped through the hand-rail, grabbed the base of a pillar with both hands and hung there.

'You'll kill yourself doing that!' the mason shouted in alarm as he reached down to grab the boy's hand. But Hei-hai pulled away, clung to a bulge in one of the bridge pylons and slid down nimbly. Pressing up against the stone like a wall lizard, he let himself down into the trough, scooped up his hammer, climbed out and disappeared under a bridge opening.

'That damned little monkey!' Director Liu said, stroking his chin. 'He's just a goddamned little monkey!'

Hei-hai emerged from under the bridge and timidly made his way to the women, who were talking and laughing. The young women blushed red as coxcombs, wanting to listen to the dirty talk, but afraid to hear it. When the boy appeared darkly in their midst, the women's mouths clamped shut. A moment later, there was a bit of whispering, and when they saw that he did not react, their voices grew louder.

'Would you look at that sorry little kid! They let him go half naked in this weather!'

'You can't love a kid that doesn't come out of you.'

'I hear she does you-know-what at home . . .'

Hei-hai turned away from the women and gazed at the river. The surface was red in places, green in others. Willow trees on the southern bank fluttered like dragonflies.

A young woman in a crimson bandana walked up behind Hei-hai and said softly, 'Where's your village, boy?'

He cocked his head and glanced at her out of the corner of his eye. He spotted a fine dusting of yellow fuzz on her upper lip. She had big eyes, but dense, fuzzy lashes gave her a sleepy look.

'What's your name, boy?'

Hei-hai was fighting with the star thistles in the sand, pinching off six- and eight-thorned thistles with his toes. Then he stepped on them, snapping off all the thorns and crushing them with feet as hard as a mule's hooves.

She laughed gaily. 'That's quite a talent, dark little boy. You have feet like horseshoes. Why don't you say something?' She poked him on the shoulder with two fingers. 'Didn't you hear me? I asked you a question.'

Hei-hai felt the two warm fingers trail down from his shoulder and stop at one of the scars on his back.

'Oh my, where did you get these?'

His ears twitched. That caught her attention, such incredibly long ears.

'So, you can wiggle your ears,' she said. 'Just like a bunny rabbit.'

Now the hand had moved up to Hei-hai's ear, and he felt the two fingers pinch his delicate lobe.

'Tell me about these scars.' She gently tugged his ear

until he was facing her, level with her chest. Rather than look up, he stared straight ahead, at red-checked fabric across which lay the tip of a yellowed braid. 'Dog bites? Boils? Climbing trees? You poor thing.'

Moved, he gazed up at her smooth, round chin. He sniffled.

'Looking to adopt, Juzi?' a large, round-faced woman shouted.

Hei-hai's eyes rolled in their sockets, the whites fluttered like moths.

'That's right, my name's Juzi,' she told him. 'I'm from a village up ahead about ten *li*. If you feel like talking, just call me "big sister Juzi".'

'Looking for a husband, Juzi? Have you found the one you want? How many years will you have to hold out till this duckling is ready to mount?'

'Stinking old crone!' Juzi cursed the fat woman. 'Nothing but shit comes out of that mouth.' She led Hei-hai over to the mountain of broken rock and dug around to find one with a flat surface. 'Sit on this,' she said, 'and stay close to me. Start breaking rocks, but take it easy.' She found a smooth rock for herself and placed it near his. In a matter of moments, the sandy area in front of the floodgate was ringing with the sound of metal on stone. With Hei-hai as their topic, the women exchanged views on a hard life and the reasons behind it. In this 'women's philosophy' eternal truths were mixed with plenty of nonsense. Juzi paid no attention to it – she was focused on the boy. At first he acknowledged her attention with an occasional glance, but before long he looked to be in a trance, eyes wide, gazing into space, while she looked on anxiously. He grasped a rock with his left hand and raised the hammer with his right. The effort seemed to exhaust him, and the hammer dropped like a heavy object in free fall. She nearly cried out every time she saw the hammer descending toward his hand, but nothing happened – the hammer traced a wobbly arc in the air, but always landed on the rock.

Hei-hai's eyes were fixed on the rocks at first, but a strange sound drifted over from the river, thin and faint, like nibbling fishes, now near, now far. Straining to capture it with both eyes and ears, he saw a bright gassy cloud rising over the river, which seemed to capture the oscillating hum within. His cheeks grew ruddy and an affecting smile gathered at the corners of his mouth. He had long forgotten where he was sitting and what he was doing, as if the arm that moved up and down belonged to someone else. Then the index finger of his left hand went numb, and the arm jerked. A sound emerged from his mouth, something between a moan and a sigh. He looked down and saw that the nail on that finger was cracked in several places, and that blood was oozing from the cracks.

'Have you smashed your finger?' the woman asked as

she jumped up and stepped over to crouch by him. 'Oh no, look what you've done! Who works like that, letting his thoughts fly off to who knows where?'

Hei-hai scooped up a handful of dirt while she was scolding him and pressed it on the injured finger.

'Have you lost your mind, Hei-hai?' She dragged him down to the river. 'There's filthy stuff in that dirt.' The soles of his feet slapped loudly on the gleaming banks. He crouched down at the river's edge, where the woman stuck his finger into the water. A trickle of dirty yellow formed in front of his finger. Once the dirt had washed away, red threads of blood quivered in the water. The boy's fingernail looked like cracked jade.

'Does it hurt?'

He didn't make a sound. His eyes were fixed on river shrimp at the bottom. The transparent crustaceans' feelers fluttered slowly, exquisitely.

She took out a handkerchief embroidered with a China rose and wrapped it around the finger, then led him back to the rock pile. 'Sit here and relax,' she said. 'No one will bother you, you poor little devil.'

The other women stopped what they were doing to cast misty looks their way. Silence lay over the rock pile. Patches of cloud floated through the bright blue sky like lambs, casting fleeting shadows that enshrouded the pale riverbank and the stoic water. The women's faces wore dreary looks, like barren soil in which nothing grew. After a long moment of indecision they went back to work, as if waking from a dream, the monotonous sound of metal on stone creating an aura of resignation.

Hei-hai sat silently, staring at the red flower embroidered on the handkerchief. Another red flower adorned the edge, this one created by blood from under his fingernail. The women quickly put him out of their minds and went back to laughing and talking. Hei-hai brought his injured finger to his mouth and untied the knot in the handkerchief with his teeth, then packed the finger in another handful of dirt. Juzi was about to say something, but stopped when she saw him retie the handkerchief around the finger using his teeth and free hand. She sighed, raised her hammer and brought it down hard on a dark red rock. Its knife-like edges emitted enormous sparks when they came in contact with the hammer, visible even in the bright sunlight.

At noon, Liu Taiyang rode out from Hei-hai and the mason's village on a black bicycle. Standing in front of the floodgate, he blew his whistle to stop work and announced that the field kitchen was up, but only available to those who lived farther than five *li*. Everyone hurriedly gathered up their tools. The young woman stood up. So did the boy.

'How far away do you live, Hei-hai?'

Hei-hai ignored her, turning his head this way and that, as if searching for something. Juzi's head followed, and when his stopped swivelling, so did hers. Looking straight ahead, her eyes met the lively eyes of the mason, and they held the look for nearly a minute.

'Time to eat, Hei-hai,' the mason said. 'Let's go home. Don't give me that look, it won't do you any good. We live a couple of *li* from here, and we're not lucky enough to eat in the kitchen.'

'You two are from the same village?' she asked the mason.

Stuttering with excitement, he pointed toward his village, telling her that he and Hei-hai lived just across the bridge. They chatted cordially, about ordinary things. He knew she lived in the village up ahead, so she could eat in the kitchen and sleep under the bridge. She was willing to eat in the kitchen, but not to sleep under the bridge. The autumn winds were too cold. She lowered her voice and asked if Hei-hai was a mute. Absolutely not, he assured her, adding that he was very intelligent, and at the age of four or five had been a real chatterbox, his crisp voice, like a bean in a bamboo tube, hardly ever stopped. But over time he spoke less and less, and often froze like a statue; no one had any idea what he was thinking. Look at his eyes, so black you can't see the bottom. The woman remarked that he did seem smart, and for some reason she'd taken a liking to him, almost like a kid brother. The mason said that's because you're a good person with a kind heart.

The three of them – mason, woman, Hei-hai – lagged behind, the man and woman talking fervently, as if hoping to drag out the walk. Hei-hai followed, lifting his legs high and stepping lightly, his expression and movements like those of a small tomcat patrolling the base of a wall. Liu Taiyang, who had been delayed in the grove of river locusts, caught up with them on his creaky bicycle when they reached the bridge, which was so narrow he had to get off and walk.

'What are you hanging around here for? How'd you do this morning, you dark little monkey? Hey, what happened to your paw?'

'Smashed his finger with the hammer.'

'Shit! Mason, go see your team leader and have him send somebody else. I won't be responsible if the kid kills himself.'

'It's a work injury,' the woman complained. 'You can't do that.'

'You and I have known each other for years, Director Liu,' the mason said. 'What's one kid for a big project like this? And what can he do in the production team with that hand?'

'Damn you, you skinny little monkey.' Director Liu mulled it over. 'I'll give you a new job. You can pump a bellows for the blacksmiths, how's that? Think you can handle it?'

The boy sent pleading looks to the mason and the woman.

'You can do that, can't you, Hei-hai?' he asked.

She pitched in with an encouraging nod.

Chapter Two

By the fifth day of pumping bellows, Hei-hai's skin had taken on the sheen and colour of fine coal. The only parts of his body that remained white were his teeth and eyes, which made his eyes more expressive than ever. When he looked at you, with his lips clamped shut, you felt as if your heart had been seared. Coal ash filled the creases next to his nose, and his hair, which had grown half an inch, was layered with the black stuff. By this time, everyone at the worksite was calling him Hei-hai – Dark Boy – and he ignored them all, and he ignored them all, wouldn't even look them in the eye. Only when Juzi or the mason spoke to him would he respond with his eyes. Everyone had stopped for lunch the day before, when a blacksmith's ball-peen hammer and a new bucket for quenching steel were stolen. Liu Taiyang stepped up onto the floodgate and railed at the people for half an hour, after which he gave Hei-hai a new job: each day at noon, when the others were eating, he was to remain at the worksite and keep watch over the tools. The blacksmith would bring him food. Director Liu said the little mutt was getting a free lunch out of it.

The crowd broke up, and the worksite that had been buzzing all morning fell eerily silent. Hei-hai walked out from under the bridge and slowly paced the sandy ground in front of the floodgate, arms behind his back, one hand on each buttock, his brows knitted beneath three creases in his forehead. Back and forth he walked, counting the bridge openings. Bubbles formed and popped in the space between his lips. He stopped at the seventh pylon, wrapped his legs around the diamond-shaped pylon rock and began shimmying up. About halfway to the top, he slid back down, raking a big patch of skin off his belly, from which beads of blood oozed. He reached down, scooped up a handful of dirt and rubbed it on the skin. Then he backed up a couple of steps, shaded his eyes with his hand and studied the seam where the pylon met the underside of the bridge. He relaxed.

He ran to where the women were breaking rocks. The one he'd sat on was no longer there. He went unerringly to the place where Juzi had been working, recognising it by the six-sided head of her hammer. He sat on her rock, constantly in motion, changing positions, until he had a direct line of sight to the seventh pylon. Having found the position he wanted, he fixed his stare on the object in the seam.

At noon Hei-hai ran over to the floodgate and hunkered down by the westernmost bridge opening. He let his eyes roam over the forge, the tongs, the sledge, the ball-peen hammer, the bucket, the shovel, every hunk of coal, even the coal chips. When it was time for the others to return to work, he picked up the coal shovel with his right hand, opened the door to the forge and started pumping the bellows with his left hand, sending a cloud of coal smoke into his eyes, which he rubbed hard, turning the blood-streaked sockets purple. The bellows, newly packed with chicken feathers, were heavy, almost too much for one hand. He banged his injured finger, and when he looked down, he was reminded of the handkerchief it was wrapped in. It was no longer white, though the embroidered China rose was still red. Visited by a new thought, he walked out from under the bridge and looked around. At the seventh pylon, he unwrapped the handkerchief, put it between his teeth and started climbing. When he'd struggled to the top, he stuck it into the seam . . .

He poked and jabbed, but the fire was out. Sweat dotted his forehead. Footsteps sounded beyond the opening, and he backed away, terrified, until he was up against the cold stone wall. He watched as a stumpy-legged young man entered the opening at a crouch, apparently intended to show that the archway was low and that he was tall. Hei-hai drew back his lips. The stumpy young man looked at the now cold forge, partially opened the bellows, then let his eyes fall on Hei-hai, up against the wall. 'You little son of a bitch,' he cursed. 'What do you think you're doing? The fire's out and the bellows are crooked. You're just looking for a beating, little bastard!' Hei-hai heard the sound of wind overhead. He felt a hard-edged hand swish above him, followed by a crisp smack, like a frog being thrown against a wall.

'Go back to breaking rocks, you little prick,' he cursed.

Hei-hai knew that this was the blacksmith, a young man with a pimply face and a nose as flat as a calf's, covered with sweat. Hei-hai watched as he deftly put the forge back in order. Then he watched him gather up golden wheat stalks from the corner, stuff them into the forge, light them, and, by gently pumping the bellows, produce wispy white smoke, followed by flames. The blacksmith shovelled in a thin layer of wet coal without letting the bellows stop. Another layer of coal was followed by yet another. Now the choking smoke was burnt brown and reeked of coal. He poked at the coal with his shovel, creating bright red flames. The coal was burning.

Hei-hai uttered an excited cry.

'You still here, you little prick?'

A tall, slight old man ambled into the opening. 'I thought the fire was banked,' he said to the young blacksmith. 'Why'd you bring it up again?' The voice rumbled, the words sounding as if they emerged from somewhere below the old man's diaphragm.

'This little prick put it out.' He pointed at Hei-hai with his shovel.

'Let him pump the bellows,' the old man said. He wrapped a yellow oilskin apron around his waist, then two more pieces around his ankles to protect his feet. All were covered with holes from hot sparks. Hei-hai knew this was the old blacksmith.

'Let him pump the bellows, so you can concentrate on your hammer. That way you won't have to work so hard.'

'Let a little kid like him pump the bellows?' the young blacksmith muttered unhappily. 'He's so monkey-skinny, the forge will bake him into kindling.'

Liu Taiyang burst in on them. 'What's the problem?' he asked with a look of exasperation. 'Didn't you say you wanted someone for the bellows?'

'Not this one! Just look at him, Director Liu, he's so skinny I doubt he could lift a fucking coal shovel. Why'd you send him to me? That's like adding rotten food to a plate just to make it look full.'

'I know exactly what's on your devious mind. You were hoping I'd send you a woman to do it, weren't you? The prettiest one of the bunch, maybe? How about the one in the crimson bandana? Fat chance, you dog turd! Hei-hai, pump the bellows.' He turned back to the blacksmith. 'You can teach him, damn it!'

Hei-hai walked timidly over to the bellows, but his eyes were on the old blacksmith's face, looking almost expectant. He noticed that the old man's face was the colour of burnt wheat, and that the bulb of his nose looked like a ripe haw berry. He came up and began teaching Hei-hai the basics of pumping a bellows; the boy's ears twitched as he took in every word.

At first he fumbled with the bellows and was sweating heavily; the heat from the flames pricked his skin painfully. The old blacksmith's face was expressionless, hard as a broken tile. He didn't so much as look at Hei-hai, who bit his lip and wiped the sweat from his face with a sunburned arm before it ran into his eyes. His gaunt chest rose and fell like the bellows; puffs of air burst from his mouth and his nostrils.

The mason carried in blunt-nosed chisels to be repaired. 'Can you hold out?' he asked Hei-hai. 'If not, tell me, and you can go back to the rock pile.'

Hei-hai didn't so much as look up.

'Pig-headed kid!' the mason said as he dumped the chisels on the ground and walked off. But he was back shortly, now in company with Juzi. She had tied her bandana around her neck; it framed her face perfectly.

Under the bridge, a light shone in the young

blacksmith's eyes; he swallowed hard, licking his dry, chapped lips with a thickened tongue. His eyes were as big as Hei-hai's, but the right one was covered by an eggshell-coloured film. Over time he'd come to rely on his left eye, leading to a habit of cocking his head to the right. With his head pillowed on his right shoulder, he sent a burning gaze from his left eye to the woman's rosy face. An eighteen-pound sledge stood between his legs, head on the ground; he rested his hand on the handle as if it were a cane.

The fire in the forge blazed, sending black smoke and sparks up to the bridge, where it swirled and returned angrily to enshroud the boy's face. He coughed, his chest wheezed. The old blacksmith gave him a frosty look, took a pipe from a leather pouch that had been rubbed shiny, slowly filled and lit it from the forge, and blew two streams of white smoke into the black cloud, making his nose hairs twitch. He cast an indifferent gaze through the smoke at the mason and Juzi. 'Not so much coal,' he said to Hei-hai. 'Nice, even layers.'

The boy frantically pumped the bellows, his skeletal figure rocking back and forth. Flames shone on his sweaty chest, throwing his ribs into clear relief. His heart beat pathetically, like a tiny mouse tucked between a pair of ribs. 'Make long, steady motions,' the old blacksmith said.

Juzi's eyes filled with tears when she noticed the

blood on Hei-hai's lower lip. 'Hei-hai,' she shouted, 'don't work for them. Come back with me to break rocks.' She walked up to the bellows and grabbed his kindling-stick arms. He fought to break her grip, and made throaty noises that sounded like the growl of a dog about to bite. He was so light she had no trouble dragging him out of the opening. His calloused feet scraped noisily across the rocky soil.

'Hei-hai,' she said as she set him down, 'let's not work for them. The smoke's too much for you. You're so skinny there isn't a drop of sweat left in you – you're baked dry. Come break rocks with your big sister, that's much easier.' She pulled him back toward the rock pile. She had strong arms and large, soft hands that enveloped his wrist as if it were a twig. Hei-hai's heels ploughed furrows in the rocky soil. 'Stop that, you foolish little boy,' she stopped to say. 'Walk with me.' She tightened her grip on his wrist. 'You're so skinny, I could shatter your bone with a squeeze, so how could you take on that kind of hard work?' Hei-hai gave her a nasty look, then dropped his head and sank his teeth into her fleshy wrist. 'Ow!' she cried out, and let go of his wrist. Hei-hai spun around and ran back to the bridge.

His teeth left deep imprints on her wrist. His canines, practically fangs, had drilled two bloody holes in her skin. The troubled mason ran up and took out a wrinkled handkerchief to wrap around her bleeding wrist.

She shoved him away, wouldn't even look at him, as she bent down, scooped up a handful of dirt, and smeared it over the bite marks.

'That's got germs!' he shouted, startled.

She turned and walked over to the rock pile, sat in her place and stared at the endless ripples on the river. She didn't break a single rock.

The women commenced whispering.

'Look, another one's turned dumb.'

'I'll bet Hei-hai knows black magic.'

'Get your ass over here, Hei-hai, you little prick,' the mason called out as he walked toward the bridge. 'How could you bite a friendly hand?'

At that moment, a bucketful of hot, dirty water flew into the mason's face. He was standing in the right spot, the aim was perfect, and not a drop of the water was wasted. His soft brown hair, his jacket and the upturned collar of his red athletic shirt were coated with iron filings and coal dust. The filthy water ran from his head in rivulets.

'Are you fucking blind?' he stormed into the opening. 'Who did that? Speak up. Who was it?'

No response. The black smoke had dissipated; the fire in the forge was blazing. The old blacksmith, his skin crimson, was taking a white-hot chisel out of the forge with a set of tongs. Sparks of molten steel popped off the tip. He laid it on the anvil and tapped the edges with his hammer. The anvil answered crisply. With the tongs in his left hand, he turned and moved the chisel, hitting it with his ball-peen hammer. The one-eyed blacksmith's sledge came down hard on each spot the older man's hammer hit, moving like a chicken pecking at rice; the younger man's sledge gave no ground.

Hot air swirled. Amid the frightful sound of steel being tempered, sparks sprayed from the chisel and landed on the oilskin aprons and foot protectors, where they sizzled and gave off white smoke. They also landed on Hei-hai's bare skin. He grimaced, baring two rows of white wolf cub teeth. Blisters rose on his belly, but he gave no sign of feeling pain, and hypnotic flames danced in his eyes. His thin shoulders hunched, his neck tucked down between them, and with his arms folded in front, he cupped his hand over his mouth and chin so tightly his nose was a mass of wrinkles.

A point was pounded onto a blunt chisel as its colour cooled from dusky red to silver grey. The ground was covered with white slag, hot enough to ignite straw, which disgorged lazy threads of white smoke.

'Who splashed me, damn it!' the mason roared in the face of the young blacksmith.

'It was me, so what!' The blacksmith said, cocking his head elegantly; his body seemed to glow as he stood with his hands on his sledge handle.

'Are you blind?'

'Only the one eye. I flung the water, and you walked into it. Just your luck.'

'That's a ridiculous argument!'

'These days the bigger fists win the argument.' He clenched his fists, making his muscles bulge.

'Come on, then, one-eyed ogre. I'll put the light out of the other one,' the mason said, drawing up threateningly. The old blacksmith approached innocently, and bumped into the mason, who sensed something radiating from the old man's sunken eyes, a kind of sign, and his muscles went slack. The old man looked up and casually sang a line from either an opera or a popular song.

For love of your sword, your learning, your youthful virility

I followed you across the earth, wracked by storm and hunger, enduring countless hardships . . .

He sang only that much, then stopped, and it was clear that he had swallowed the melody's last mournful strains. He glanced at the mason again, then lowered his head to quench the newly sharpened chisel in the bucket; but just before he did that, he rolled up his sleeve and thrust a hand into the water to test the temperature. A deep purple scar on his forearm, round with a raised centre, did not really resemble an eye, but it looked like one to the mason, who felt that the strange eye was watching him. Twisting his lip, he felt as if a spell had been cast. He emerged from under the bridge as if walking on air, and disappeared for the rest of the day.

The boy's eyes ached, his sun-baked scalp burned. He stood up from her seat and strolled back to the forge. It was dark under the bridge, so he felt his way over to the old blacksmith's folding stool. As he sat on it, his mind a blank, his hands abruptly began to burn, so he pressed them against the cold stone wall and directed his thoughts to the past.

Three days earlier, the old blacksmith had taken time off to return home and fetch padded clothes and bedding, saying that the older you got, the more you valued your legs, and that he didn't feel like walking home after work each day. He would spread his bedding near the forge to stay warm at night. (Hei-hai eyed the blacksmith's bedding. The northern edge of the bridge opening had been sealed by a flashboard, though sunlight shone through the gaps and fell on a greasy padded jacket and mangy dog-skin bed mat.) When his master left for home, the younger one became the ruler of the forge. He entered that morning, chest thrown out, belly protruding, and announced amiably, 'Light off the forge, Hei-hai. The old guy's gone home, so it's just you and me.'

Hei-hai just stared.

'What are you gawking at, you little prick? You think

I'm not good enough? I've been with the old guy three years, I know all his tricks.'

Hei-hai lazily started a fire as the blacksmith smugly hummed a tune. He thrust several pieces of steel from the day before into the mouth of the forge. Hei-hai made the fire inside roar, adding red to the black of his face. The young blacksmith burst out laughing. 'Hei-hai,' he shouted, 'anyone would think you were a Red Army soldier, with all those scars.'

The boy pumped the bellows even harder.

'How come that foxy foster mother of yours hasn't come to see you lately? She's probably mad that you bit her. What does her arm taste like? Is it sour? Sweet? You sure know how to enjoy good food, you little fuck! Give me a chance to hold that tender arm of hers and I'd gnaw it like a cucumber.'

Hei-hai picked up the tongs, pulled a piece of white-hot steel out of the forge, and banged it down on the anvil.

'That was fast, boy!' The blacksmith picked up a medium-sized hammer, smaller than his sledge but bigger than the ball-peen, gripped the steel with his tongs, and pounded with all his might. Hei-hai stood watching. The blacksmith was strong, and his hammer seemed to have a life of its own. The pointed end of the chisel was perfectly tapered, like a newly sharpened pencil. Hei-hai looked sadly at the old blacksmith's ball-peen hammer. The younger man carried the chisel over to the bucket and quenched it in the water, his actions a mirror image of those made by the older man. Hei-hai turned away and fixed his eyes once more on the hammer lying alongside the anvil. Its wooden handle was as shiny as the horns of an old bull.

The young blacksmith worked with quick precision, and in short order had tempered a dozen or more chisels. He sat proudly on the master's stool and rolled a cigarette. After putting it between his lips, he told Hei-hai to bring him a live coal to light it. 'You see, son? We did just fine without the old guy.'

At the height of his self-satisfaction, masons who had taken the new chisels to the worksite reappeared.

'What kind of shitty work are you giving us, black-smith? The tips either break off or bend. We're working with stone out there, not bean curd. Wait till your master returns, and don't use our chisels for practice.'

They dumped the chisels on the ground and left. The blacksmith's face darkened. He shouted for Hei-hai to get the fire going again and reheat the chisels. Soon after, when he'd hammered and quenched them a second time, he personally carried them to the worksite. But he'd no sooner returned to the bridge than the masons followed, dumping more ruined chisels on the ground and raining curses on his head. 'You pathetic fuck, quit messing with us. Look at your work! Every fucking tip has broken off!'

Hei-hai looked at the blacksmith, wrinkles appearing at the corners of his mouth, though it was impossible to tell if he was happy or sad. The blacksmith flung his tools away, crouched down and sulked. As he smoked a cigarette, his good eye rolled in its socket, resulting in a puzzled, angry stare, his eyebrows wriggling like tadpoles. He flicked his cigarette butt away and stood up.

'Shit!' he said. 'Light a fire, Hei-hai, and let's get back at it.'

Hei-hai pumped the bellows lethargically. The blacksmith exhorted and cursed him, but he didn't look up. The steel was hot. The blacksmith struck it a couple of times and then carried it over to the water bucket. But this time, instead of quenching the steel gradually, like the old master did, he dunked it all the way in; the water sizzled and released a twisting cloud of steam. He lifted the chisel out of the water, held it up and cocked his head to examine the pattern and colour. He then laid it on the anvil and rapped it lightly with his hammer, splitting the steel in half. Dejected, he threw his hammer to the ground and flung one half of the steel as far as he could outside the bridge opening, where it landed on a rock. It looked ugly.

'Go pick that up,' he barked at Hei-hai. The boy's ears twitched, but his legs stayed put. For this he received a kick in the pants, a bang on the shoulder with a pair of tongs and a deafening shout in the ear: 'Go bring that thing back to me!'

Head down, Hei-hai walked over to the chisel, bent over slowly and picked it up. It sizzled in his hand. There was a smell of fried pork. The chisel thudded to the ground.

The blacksmith could hardly believe his eyes. He burst out laughing. 'I forgot it was still hot, you little prick. Your trotter is cooked. Let's eat!'

Hei-hai walked back to the bridge opening, ignoring the blacksmith as he thrust his scalded hand into the bucket of water. Then he walked slowly out from under the bridge and bent over to examine the broken chisel. It was silvery with a rough, pitted surface. The muddy ground on which it lay was steaming: a thin, almost invisible whiteness. He bent lower until his rear end was sticking up in the air; his shorts hiked up to expose thighs that were much lighter in colour than his calves. One of his hands rested on his back, the other hung straight down and swung closer to the chisel, water dripping onto it from his fingertips. Each drop hissed and bounced noisily as it shrank to form a pattern, smaller and smaller until it disappeared. He felt the heat on the tips of his fingers, heat that made its way through his chest and into his heart.

'What the hell are you doing there, bent double with

your ass in the air like a pilloried capitalist roader?' the blacksmith yelled at him.

Hei-hai's hand shook as he picked up the chisel; then, grabbing his behind with his left hand, he sauntered back. When the blacksmith saw yellow smoke rising from Hei-hai's hand, his eye seemed riveted. 'Let go of it!' the blacksmith shouted. 'Drop it!' His voice now sounded like the screech of a cat. 'Drop it, you little prick!'

Hei-hai crouched down in front of the blacksmith, opened his hand and shook it a couple of times. The chisel rolled twice and stopped at the blacksmith's feet. He stayed on his haunches as he looked up into the blacksmith's face.

'Stop looking at me, you son of a bitch, stop it!' The blacksmith was trembling. He looked away. Hei-hai stood up and walked out from under the bridge.

He recalled looking into the cloudless western sky after he emerged. A white half-moon hung in the sky like a tiny cloud.

He was worn out from thinking. There was a buzzing in his ears. He got up from the old blacksmith's stool, and went over and lay down on the man's bedding. He pillowed his head on the jacket, and his eyes drifted closed. He felt someone caressing his face and his hands. It hurt, but he bore it. Two drops of water fell heavily, one onto his lips, which he swallowed, the other onto his nose, which stung.

'Wake up, Hei-hai, have something to eat.'

His nose ached terribly. He clambered to his feet and saw her. Tears threatened to spill from his eyes, but he forced them back down.

'Here,' she said as she untied her crimson bandana. It held two corn buns, one with a piece of pickled cucumber folded into it, the other a leek. A long strand of her bleach-tipped black hair lay across the buns. She picked it up with two fingers and flicked it away, where it landed with a sound that reverberated in Hei-hai's ears.

'Eat up, you little mutt,' she said as she rubbed his neck.

The boy kept his eyes on her as he bit into the buns and chewed.

'How did you burn your hand? Did that one-eyed dragon do that to you? Are you going to bite me again? You've got sharp fangs.'

The boy's ears flapped like fans. He raised a bun in his left hand and the leek and the cucumber in his right, and covered his face.

Chapter Three

A thundershower struck that night. When the workers showed up the next morning, they saw that the rocks had been washed clean and the sandy ground levelled. Water in the trough was twice as high as the day before; the few remaining clouds were reflected in the brilliant blue water. There was a sudden chill in the air; the autumn wind bored through the bridge openings and, together with the rustling of the sea of jute plants, chilled people from the inside out. The old blacksmith's padded jacket, shiny as armour, was missing its buttons, and he could only close it by drawing together the lapels and securing them with a red plastic-wrapped electric cord. Hei-hai, still wearing only a pair of shorts, was bare-chested and barefoot, but he didn't seem to suffer from the cold. A red plastic-wrapped electric cord also held up his shorts, in place of the cloth sash he'd either lost or put away. His hair had grown wild and was now two inches long, every strand standing up like the spines of a hedgehog. The workers looked at him with pity and admiration as he walked over the rocky ground, with its pooled rainwater, in bare feet.

'Aren't you cold?' the old blacksmith asked.

Hei-hai gave a confused look, as if he hadn't understood the question.

'I asked you if you're cold,' the blacksmith repeated, raising his voice a bit. The look of confusion disappeared as Hei-hai lowered his head and began lighting the forge. He lightly pumped the bellows with his left hand, holding the coal shovel in his right, and stared at the burning stalks of wheat. The old blacksmith took his greasy jacket off the bed and draped it over Hei-hai's back. The boy squirmed with obvious discomfort. As soon as the blacksmith walked off, Hei-hai took off the jacket and laid it back on the bed. With a shake of his head, the old man crouched down to smoke.

'No wonder you like to stay close to the forge,' the young blacksmith said with a bored yawn. 'That's how you keep warm. Shit, you might be little, but you're cunning as hell.'

A whistle sounded at the worksite. Deputy Director Liu called everyone together. The workers gathered in front of the floodgate, facing the sun, the men standing with their arms folded, the women stitching shoe soles. Hei-hai stole an uneasy look at the seam above the seventh bridge pylon. The weather's turning cold, Director

Liu said, so we're going to have to put in overtime and pour concrete for the foundation before the freeze sets in. Starting today, overtime will be from seven to ten at night. You'll earn half a *jin* of grain and twenty cents each day. No one complained, though there were as many different expressions as there were faces – more than two hundred of them. Hei-hai watched the mason's pale face turn red and then purple, while the woman's ruddy face blanched, first grey, then white.

That night three gas lamps illuminated the worksite. One lit the areas where the masons worked, a second the area where the women broke rocks. Most of them had children and plenty of housework at home, so they gave up the half a *jin* of grain and twenty cents. No more than a dozen young women stayed to work under the artificial light. Since their homes were far from the worksite, they gathered their courage and slept squeezed together under one of the arched openings, after sealing both ends with flashboards, leaving a narrow opening in front through which they climbed in and out. Juzi sometimes slept with the other women, at other times she went to the village (a cousin whose husband had a temporary job in the county town and didn't always come home at night had invited her to sleep there).

The third lamp threw its light on an old man, a young one, and a boy near the forge. The sound of steel on rock rang from the masons' worksite, where chisels gave off sparks as they chewed up rock. The men worked hard. The mason took off his jacket; his red athletic shirt shone like a lit torch. The younger women sat around their gas lamp, their minds filled with pleasant fancies. At times they laughed out loud, and at times they whispered among themselves amid the intermittent cracks of breaking rock. The sound of the flowing river filled gaps between the noises they made. Juzi lay down her hammer, stood up, and stole toward the river. She cast a long shadow on the sandy ground. 'Watch out some hot-blooded bachelor doesn't grab you,' a woman behind her called out. She walked quickly out of the circle of light. Each ray appeared to her as a bright white ball with thorns stretching toward her, but falling short. The tips of the thorns were red, and soft. Later she walked back toward the light; she had a sudden desire to see what Hei-hai was doing. Avoiding the lamplight, she stepped into the shadow of the first bridge pylon.

There she spotted him, moving like a little sprite, the radiant light spreading across his bare back like a coat of glaze. His skin resembled smooth rubber, elastic yet tough, durable and impenetrable. He appeared to have put on weight, for now there was something between his skin and his ribs. And no wonder, since she brought him lunch from the kitchen every day. He went home to sleep at night, but seldom to eat, and some nights he didn't go back at all – one morning she saw him emerge from under the bridge with straw in his hair.

He pumped the bellows so smoothly it was as if it were moving his hands rather than the other way around. His body rocked back and forth, his head looking like a watermelon floating on a lazy river. Bright glints in his black eyes bobbed up and down, like dancing fireflies.

The young blacksmith stood in his customary pose next to the chisels, holding his sledge in both hands, head cocked to the side, his good eye staring straight ahead, like a contemplative rooster.

The old blacksmith removed a heated chisel from the forge; Hei-hai took a ruined one and laid it in its place. The heated chisels were white tinged with green. The old blacksmith laid the chisel on the anvil and tapped the side of the anvil with his ball-peen hammer. The younger man lazily raised his sledge, twirled it in the air, as if it were a jute stalk, and let it fall gently onto the hot steel, sending sparks of molten steel flying in all directions. They burst into smaller sparks as they hit the wall. Some landed on Hei-hai's slightly bulging belly, bouncing off softly and tracing lovely arcs of light before falling to the ground. As the sparks met his belly and fell to the ground, their friction with the air created heat and sound. After the first strike with his sledge, the young blacksmith flexed his muscles, as if he'd been suddenly awakened, and began to move faster. Juzi saw strange shadows dancing on the rocky wall and heard the *clang, clang, clang* of metal on metal. The blacksmith's ability to shape steel was exceptional, and the hammer in the old man's hand had nothing to do but tap the anvil. The young man knew precisely where to aim. The old master turned chisels on the anvil, his eyes and thoughts lighting on the spots to strike, and the young man's sledge landed there an instant later, sometimes anticipating the older man.

Juzi was awestruck by the young man's skill, though she also kept an eye on the boy and the old blacksmith. Hei-hai stood numbly by when the hammering was at its most impressive (eyes shut, breathing in time with the bellows); that was also a sad moment for the old blacksmith, as if each swing of the young man's sledge was aimed not at the chisels but at his dignity.

When the chisel was shaped, the old man turned to quench it in the bucket. He cast a meaningful glance at the younger man, the corners of his mouth turning down disdainfully. The younger man watched his master's every move. The woman saw the older blacksmith test the water with his hand, then raise the chisel to examine it before bending over, shrimp-like, looking closely at the water in the bucket, and tentatively dipping in the tip. The water sizzled and sent a fine steam into the air, where it enveloped the old man's red nose.

After a moment, he again raised the chisel to his eyes, as if preparing to thread a needle, as if a wonderful design were painted there. He was obviously happy with what he saw, as the wrinkles on his face filled with pleasure. He nodded, seemingly having received the response he'd hoped for, then buried the chisel in the water. Steam billowed, a mushroom cloud that filled the bridge opening, turning the gaslight red and the other objects into a shifting blur. All returned to normal when the steam dissipated: Hei-hai still dreamily pumped the bellows; the young blacksmith remained in his customary contemplative rooster pose; and the old blacksmith – his date-like face, black enamel eyes, and arms with scars like dung beetles – had not moved.

The old blacksmith picked up a second chisel, and everything began again, right up to the moment when he was about to quench it – then something changed. After testing the water, he added cold water, and looked satisfied. Just as he was about to put the chisel in, the young blacksmith bounded over to the bucket and stuck his right hand in. Without a second thought, the old man thrust the chisel against the younger man's right forearm. The smell of burning flesh surged from under the bridge, straight into the woman's nostrils.

The young blacksmith screeched in pain, straightened up, and, with a nasty grin, shouted, 'It's been three years, Master!'

The old man dropped the chisel into the bucket, roiling the water inside and once again filling the opening with steam. Juzi could not see their faces in the mist, but she heard the old man say: 'Remember this!'

She ran off before the mist cleared, clamping her hand over her mouth to keep down the bitter juices churning in her stomach. As she sat before the rock pile, one of the women teased her: 'You've been gone a long time, Juzi. Out with that boy in the jute field?' Juzi did not respond, letting the ridicule pass. She pinched her throat with two fingers to keep from making a sound.

The whistle to stop work blew. Juzi had been caught up in her thoughts for three hours. 'Thinking about a man, Juzi? Let's go,' they called to her. But she sat there watching figures move in the hazy light.

'Juzi.' The young mason was standing behind her. 'Your cousin asked me to give you a message. She wants you to spend the night at her place. I'll go with you, all right?'

'Go? Who are you talking to?'

'I'm talking to you. What's the matter? Are you sick?'

'Is who sick?'

'I'm talking about you.'

'Well, don't.'

'Shall we go?'

'OK.'

The water passed noisily under the bridge. Juzi stopped. The mason was only a step away from her. Turning to look, she saw light emerge from the opening at the westernmost pylon. The other two gaslights had been extinguished. She began walking toward the floodgate.

'Looking for Hei-hai?'

'I want to see him.'

'Let's go together. The little bastard. Be careful, don't fall off the bridge.'

Juzi sensed that the mason was close; she could hear his heartbeat. They walked and walked, and as her head tilted to the side, it came to rest on his powerful shoulder. She leaned back and was immediately embraced by a muscular arm. He reached over, cupped the little mound of her breast with his big hand, and stroked it. Her heart beat frantically beneath that breast, like a fluttering pigeon. They walked steadily toward the floodgate. When they entered the circle of light, she removed his hand from her breast and, sensibly, he let his arm drop.

'Hei-hai!' she shouted.

'Hei-hai!' he echoed her.

The young blacksmith looked at both of them with his good eye; his cheek twitched. The old blacksmith was sitting on his bed, holding his pipe in both hands, as if it were a pistol. He glanced at Juzi – dark red – and then the mason – pale yellow – and said in a weary but kindly tone, 'Sit down and wait, he'll be right back.'

Empty water bucket in hand, Hei-hai climbed up the levee.

When the workday had ended earlier that day, the young blacksmith had stretched lazily and said, 'I'm famished. Hei-hai, take a bucket to the north field. Dig up some sweet potatoes and pick some radishes for a late-night snack.'

Sleepy-eyed, Hei-hai looked at the old blacksmith, who was sitting on his bed, looking like a defeated rooster with its feathers ruffled.

'What are you gawking at, you little son of a bitch?' the young one demanded, straightening up and stretching his neck. 'Do as I tell you.' His good eye swept across his master, collapsed on his bed. Pain shot through the burn on his arm, but the pleasure that arm had brought him overcame the pain, and the temperature was just right, absolutely wonderful.

Hei-hai shuffled off with his empty bucket. As he emerged from the bridge opening it was as if he'd fallen into a well with a thump; he was enshrouded in such utter darkness that hazy lights flared in his eyes. He crouched down fearfully and shut them. When he opened them again, the sky had changed – now starlight fell warmly upon him and on the dark grey ground all around.

On the levee, branches of the river locusts stretched

and intertwined. He reached up to part them with one hand, then hunched his shoulders and walked up the slope. His hand brushed against the full, ripe seedpods on the damp tips of branches; the pungent scent of the branches assailed him. His foot bumped into something soft and warm, and he heard a chirp. Before he realised that it was a bamboo partridge, the bird had flapped its way out of the brush and landed in a jute field like a dark stone. Feeling somewhat guilty, he touched the spot where the bird had been resting with his foot. It was dry, a clump of dry grass that still retained the bird's warmth. From where he stood on the levee he heard the woman and the mason shout his name. He banged on the side of his bucket, and the shouts stopped. He heard the river rushing forward brightly, and the screech of an owl on a tree somewhere in the village. His stepmother was afraid of two things: thunder and the screech of an owl. He wished there were thunder every day, and a screeching owl at his stepmother's window every night. The dew on the river locusts wetted his arms, which he wiped dry on his shorts as he crossed the levee road and started down the other side. By then he'd gotten used to the dark and could see clearly, could even distinguish the subtle difference between the brown of the soil at his feet and the purple of the sweet potato leaves. He crouched down, pulled up one of the sweet potatoes and tossed it into his bucket, where it rattled around.

He dug some more, until he felt something drop off his finger, and heard it bounce off a sweet potato leaf. Feeling his left hand with the right, he discovered that the damaged fingernail had fallen off. By now his bucket was heavy, so he stood up and headed north. When he reached the radish field, he picked six in a row, twisted off the leafy tops, threw them to the ground and tossed the radishes into his bucket.

'What have you done with Hei-hai?' the mason demanded of the young blacksmith.

'What are you worried about? He's not your son, is he?'

'Where is he?' Juzi asked, boring her eyes into the blacksmith's.

'Just hold on.' he said amiably. 'He's out scrounging sweet potatoes. Stick around; we'll bake some when he gets back.'

'You sent him out to steal?'

'What do you mean, steal? It's not stealing if he doesn't take them home,' the blacksmith explained.

'Then why didn't you do it?'

'I'm his mentor.'

'That's horseshit!'

'So what if it is?' the blacksmith said as his eye lit up. 'Where the hell did you go for sweet potatoes, Hei-hai?' he shouted out of the bridge opening. 'Albania?'

Hei-hai, his shoulders askew, staggered in carrying

his bucket with both hands. He was covered with mud, as if he'd rolled around in the dirt.

'Hey, my boy,' the blacksmith complained loudly, 'I sent you out for a few. Who told you to bring back a bucketful? Take the radishes over to the pond to wash off the mud.'

'No,' Juzi said. 'Quit giving him orders. You bake the potatoes while I go wash the radishes.'

The blacksmith stacked the sweet potatoes next to the forge and calmly lit a fire. Juzi returned with the radishes and laid them out on a dry rock. One dropped to the ground, where it rolled to the mason's feet, quickly getting coated in iron filings. He leaned over to pick it up.

'Here, I'll go wash it again.'

'No need. Five large radishes is plenty,' the mason said as he laid the errant radish on the anvil.

Hei-hai walked up and took the bellows handle from the blacksmith. The blacksmith glanced at the woman before saying to him, 'You need a rest, you little shit. Do your palms get itchy when you're not doing something? Take the bellows, just don't say I didn't warn you. Take it slow, the slower the better. Otherwise you'll burn them.'

The mason and the woman sat against the western wall of the bridge opening, while the young blacksmith sat behind Hei-hai. The old blacksmith sat on his bed on the north side, looking south; the tobacco in his pipe had burned out, but he still held the bowl in both hands, resting his elbows on his knees.

The night deepened. Hei-hai continued gently working the bellows, the emerging air sounding like a sleeping baby's breathing. The sound of flowing water grew clearer, as if it had both shape and colour, that it could be smelled and seen. Barely visible shadows on the levee looked like small animals chasing each other. The sound of their claws in the sand as minute as fine animal hair pierced the bright river music like long, thin, silver threads. Jute plants near the floodgate brushed against each other, creating a sustained rustle. Only one gas lamp remained lit on the worksite. After a moment of confusion, the light-seeking insects that had surrounded the other two lamps swarmed toward the forge. In their frantic search for light, they peppered the glass shade of the remaining lamp with their bodies. The mason went to the lamp and pumped it with a clacking sound. A single cricket forced its way in through a crack in the lamp glass and knocked over the asbestos mantle, casting the bridge into darkness. It took them all a moment to make out faces. The air from Hei-hai's bellows made the fire in the forge ripple like soft red silk. The bridge opening was filled with the scent of baked sweet potatoes, which the young blacksmith turned over with his tongs. The aroma thickened. At last, their hands full of radish and sweet potato, they ate. Steam rose from the peeled sweet potatoes. Then one bite cold, one bite hot, one bite devoured, one bite savoured – *chomp, slurp* – beads of sweat on nose tips. The young blacksmith ate one radish and two sweet potatoes more than the others. The old blacksmith did not eat; he sat rigid as a statue.

'Are you going home, Hei-hai?' asked the woman.

Hei-hai licked the bits of sweet potatoes stuck to his lips. His belly bulged.

'Will your stepmother leave the door open for you?' the mason asked. 'You can sleep here on the wheat stalks if you want.'

Hei-hai coughed and flung a piece of potato skin into the forge, and then made it curl with a pump of his bellows. A burnt smell permeated the opening.

'What was that for, you little bastard?' the young blacksmith said. 'Why bother going home? I'll adopt you as son and apprentice. We'll roam the world together. I guarantee you'll eat good food and drink strong liquor!'

Before his voice had faded away, the strains of a melancholy song filled the bridge opening, raising goose pimples of joy on the mason's skin. He had heard the words of this song or aria only days before.

For love of your sword, your learning, your youthful virility
  I followed you across the earth, wracked by storm and hunger, enduring countless hardships . . .

The old man rested his back against the flashboard, where wind from the jute field blew through the cracks above him. Strands of white hair fluttered along with the dancing coal flame in the forge. Deep feeling played on his face; his narrow jaw muscles squirmed, his eyes were like burning coals.

> *. . . A bed shared three years, those heavenly pleasures and so much love, all trodden down like muck. I fanned you on summer nights, I warmed your feet on wintry eves. The fruits of my breast, the furnace in my belly . . . Yet you, with your high station, your bountiful land, have abandoned me for your wife's chambers. And I, I am a desolate slave . . .*

Juzi's heart was in her throat, her mouth half open, her lashes seemingly frozen on her face as she gazed at the old blacksmith's expressive face and his long neck, on which the Adam's apple slid up and down like a bead of mercury. The plaintive, brooding melody battered her heart like an autumn rain, but just as she was about to cry, the song turned spirited and expansive, and her heart fluttered like willow branches tossed in the wind. A tingling spread from her spine to the top of her head, and she instinctively leaned against the mason's shoulder, taking his large, callused hand in hers, her eyes moist with tears as she was enveloped in the old blacksmith's song, in his mood. His gaunt face burned with radiance, and she saw in it a future for her, much like that in his song.

The mason wrapped his arm around her, and again rested his large hand on her firm breast. The young blacksmith, sitting behind Hei-hai, began to squirm. He heard his master bray like an old donkey; a harsh, ugly sound. But soon he was deaf even to that. He rose up on his haunches and cocked his head; his left eye seemed to rise up with him, its gaze like a claw that scratched and gouged the woman's face. When the mason had tenderly placed his hand on the woman's breast, a fire was kindled in the young blacksmith's gut. Flames flew up into his throat and burst from his nose and mouth. It felt to him as if he were crouching on a taut spring, that if he let go he would shoot into the air to crash against the floodgate's steel and concrete surface. He held on, grinding his teeth.

Hei-hai grasped the bellows handle with both hands. The fire in the forge had weakened, and a blue and a yellow flame danced on the lumps of coal. Occasionally, the flow of air lifted the tongues of fire high above the forge bed, where they floated in the air before being brought down by human movement below. The boy, oblivious to the others, tried to train one eye on each of the tongues of fire, one yellow and the other blue, but could not manage to split his gaze into two. Disheartened, he moved his gaze from the fire and looked from side to side before fixing it on the anvil crouching in front of the forge like an enormous beast. For the first time, his mouth opened wide, and he released a sigh of emotion (a sound drowned out by the old blacksmith's song). His eyes, big and bright to begin with, now shone like searchlights as he witnessed a strange and beautiful sight: a soft blue-green light suffused the sleek surface of the anvil, on which rested a golden radish. In shape and size it was like a pear, though it had a long tail, every fibre of which was a strand of golden wool. Glittering and transparent, exquisitely limpid, its golden skin revealed a swirling silvery liquid inside. Its contours were clean and elegant; golden rays spread out from its beautiful curves, some long, some short – the long rays like beards of wheat, the short like eyelashes – and all were gold in colour.

The old blacksmith's song was pushed far into the distance, like the buzzing of a fly. Hei-hai floated past the bellows, a shadowy figure, and stood in front of the anvil. His hand, coated with coal dust, scarred and burned, trembled as he reached out . . .

The hand was but inches away from the radish when the young blacksmith raced up and kicked over a water bucket, spilling water on the ground and soaking the old blacksmith's bedding. He snatched up the radish, his good eye bloodshot. 'You fucker! Dumb dog! Lousy bitch! What makes you think you can eat a radish? I've got a fire in my belly and smoke in my throat, and this is just the thing to quench my thirst!' He opened his mouth, exposing two rows of blackened teeth, and was about to take a bite when Hei-hai, with a rare burst of speed, stuck his rail-thin arms under the man's elbows, lifted him off his feet, and then let him slide down. The radish fell to the ground. The blacksmith landed a kick on Hei-hai's behind, sending the boy into the arms of the woman. The mason reached out to catch him.

The old blacksmith stopped his hoarse singing and slowly stood up. The woman and the mason stood as well. Three pairs of eyes were fixed on the young blacksmith. Hei-hai's head was reeling, everything was spinning. He shook his head to clear it and saw the blacksmith pick up the radish and put it in his mouth. Hei-hai threw a lump of coal at him. It sailed past his cheek, hit the flashboard and landed on the old black-smith's bed.

'I'll beat the shit out of you, motherfucker!' the black-smith roared.

The mason stepped between them. 'You're not going to do anything to the boy,' he said.

'Give him back the radish,' the woman said.

'Give it back? Hell no!' The blacksmith ran out from under the bridge and threw the radish as hard as he could. It flew with a whooshing sound; after a long moment came a sound as if a rip had been made in the river's surface.

A golden rainbow arced in front of Hei-hai's eyes. He crumpled to the ground between the mason and the woman.

Chapter Four

The golden radish splashed into the river, floating on the surface for a moment before settling to the riverbed, where it rolled around until it was buried in golden sand. A heavy mist rose above the spot where it had torn the surface of the river.

In the early morning hours, the mist covered the valley; the river sobbed beneath it. Early rising ducks on the riverbank stared mournfully at the rolling mist. One of the bold ones waddled impatiently toward the water, but the curtain of mist over reeds at the water's edge blocked its way. Craning its neck left, right and straight ahead, it retreated from the spongy mist, quacking its displeasure. Eventually the sun rose and carved lanes and tunnels in the mist, through which the ducks saw an old man carrying his bedding and heavy tools over his shoulder, following the river westward. His back was badly bent, the load weighing down his shoulders and forcing his neck out ahead, swan-like. Once he was out of sight, a dark, bare-chested and barefoot boy came into view. A drake passed a meaningful look to the female next to it: Remember? It was him that time. The bucket bounced into a willow tree and rolled down to the river. He sprawled like a dog on the ground, and then went down to the river to get the nearly empty bucket; it could have killed that no-good sheldrake . . .

The female replied, Right, right, that damned sheldrake is always following me around, saying filthy things. Too bad it didn't kill him . . .

Hei-hai paced slowly along the riverbank, trying to see through the mist. He could hear ducks *quack-quacking* noisily on the opposite bank. He crouched down, rested his large head on his knees and wrapped his arms around chilled calves. The rising sun burned his back as if it were a forge.

He'd spent the night under the bridge instead of going home. When the cock crowed he heard the old blacksmith speaking loudly in the bridge opening. Then quiet had returned. Unable to go back to sleep, he'd gotten up and walked across the chilled sand to the river's edge. Seeing the old blacksmith's hunched back, he'd started walking toward him but slipped in the sand and fell on his rear. By the time he was back on his feet, the old man had disappeared in the mist.

Now he was on his haunches, watching the sun cleave the mist like a knife through bean curd. Across the river, ducks cast superior looks his way. The water came into view as a bright, silvery expanse, but to his disappointment, he could not see the bottom. There was a commotion at the worksite – Director Liu was fuming: 'Shit, something crazy happened at the forge. The old bastard rolled up his bedding and took off without a word to anyone. The little bastard is gone too. What happened to organisational discipline?'

'Hei-hai!'

'Hei-hai!'

'Isn't that him crouching by the water?'

Juzi and the mason ran over and picked him up by the arms.

'Why are you crouching here, you poor thing?' she asked as she picked straw from his scalp. 'It's too cold to be doing that.'

'There are sweet potatoes left over from last night. Get old one-eye to bake them for you.'

'The old blacksmith's gone,' Juzi said sombrely.

'He *is* gone.'

'Now what? Should we let him stay with the other one? What if he mistreats him?'

'Don't worry about that, the boy can take anything. Besides, we're here, so he won't do anything stupid.'

They dragged Hei-hai over to the worksite. At each step he turned to look back.

'Walk properly, you little dope,' the mason said.

'What's there to see in the river?' He squeezed Hei-hai's arm.

'I thought the old guy kidnapped you, you little shit,' Liu Taiyang said before turning to the young blacksmith. 'And you, since you squeezed the old guy out, make sure you keep up the work. If you don't fix the chisels for us, I'll gouge out your good eye.'

The young man smiled arrogantly. 'Wait and see, old Liu,' he said. 'But I get his wages and grain rations, or you can look for someone else.'

'We'll wait and see. If you do good work, fine. If not, you can fuck off.'

'Light a fire, son,' the blacksmith ordered Hei-hai.

Hei-hai was like a zombie all morning. His actions were erratic, his work sloppy. Sometimes he shovelled in too much coal, filling the opening with black smoke, other times he laid the chisels back end first, heating the wrong end.

'Where the fuck is your head?' the blacksmith cursed angrily. He was working up a sweat, excitement over his own skills seeping out through his pores. Hei-hai watched as he stuck his hand into the water bucket before quenching the steel. A rag covered the burn on his upper arm, which gave off a rank fishy odour. A pale cloud seemed to obscure Hei-hai's vision; he was downcast.

After nine o'clock the sunlight was beautiful; a single ray lit up the western wall of the dark bridge opening, filling the space with light. The blacksmith took the tempered chisels and personally delivered them to the masons for inspection. Hei-hai tossed away the tool in his hand and tiptoed out of the opening. The sudden brightness was just as dizzying as sudden darkness. He froze for a moment before breaking into a run, and was standing at the river's edge within seconds. The ridged dog-turd grass eyed him curiously. Purple water lilies and the brown caps of nut grass greedily sniffed the smell of coal dust on his body. The subtle aroma of water plants and the light stink of silver carp floated over from the river. His nose twitched, his lungs expanded like a turtledove's wings. The river was white, shot with black and purple. His eyes stung, but he kept staring, as if to penetrate the quicksilver sheen on the surface. Then he hiked up his shorts, tested the water and sort of danced in. At first the water came up only to his knees, but it quickly reached his thighs. He hiked his shorts all the way up, exposing his grape-coloured buttocks. He was now standing in the middle of the river. Sunlight from all directions rained down on him, painted his body, bored into his black eyes and turned them the colour of green bananas at the dam. The river flowed swiftly, each wave striking him in the legs. He was on hard sand, but soon the water washed it out from under his feet and he was standing in a hollow, his shorts soaked, half stuck to his legs and half floating behind him, dyeing the water around him black from coal dust. Sand churning at his feet caressed his calves. Two amber-coloured drops of water hung on his cheeks, and the corners of his mouth twitched. He walked around in the water, feeling the bottom with his feet, seeking, searching.

'Hei-hai! Hei-hai!' The mason was calling him from the bridge opening. 'You'll drown out there, Hei-hai.'

He heard the blacksmith come up to the riverbank, but didn't turn to look. All the man could see was the boy's green back.

'Come out of there!' the blacksmith said, picking up a dirt clod and throwing it; it sailed over Hei-hai's head, brushing the tips of his hair before falling into the water to create oval ripples. A second clod hit him in the back. He fell forward, his lips touching the water. He spun around and, huffing and wheezing, waded fitfully toward the river's edge. He stood in front of the blacksmith, dripping wet. His shorts stuck to his skin, his little pecker sticking up like a silkworm chrysalis. The blacksmith raised his bear-like paw to slap him, but suddenly felt as if a cat's claw had scored his heart. The boy's eyes never left his face.

'Go stoke the fire. My chisels are as good as the old guy's,' he said proudly, patting Hei-hai on the nape of his neck.

During an idle moment at the forge, the blacksmith put the sweet potatoes from the night before into the forge to bake. A light wind blew in from the jute fields. Sunlight shone straight into the arched openings. The blacksmith singing as he turned the sticky potatoes over with his tongs.

From Beijing to Nanjing, I've never seen anyone string up an electric light in their pants.

'Have you ever seen that, Hei-hai? How about your adopted mother's pants?' That reminded him. 'Run over and pick some radishes,' he said. 'When you bring them back, I'll give you a couple of potatoes.'

Hei-hai's eyes lit up, and the blacksmith saw his heart leap in the space between his ribs. The boy took off like a jackrabbit before the man could say another word. As he clambered up the levee, Hei-hai heard Juzi call his name in the distance. He turned to look, but was blinded by the sun. He ran down the other side and into the jute field. The plants were scattered across the field, no columns or rows. Where more seeds had landed, the stalks were thin, like fingers or pencils; where there were fewer plants, they were as thick as sickle handles or arms. But they were all the same height. Looking out from atop the levee, it was like gazing at a gently rippling lake. Now he parted the plants as he moved, suffering the onslaught of thorns and sending mature leaves to the ground. Quickly arriving at a spot parallel to the radish field, he turned and headed west. When he neared the field, he fell to his hands and knees and began to crawl; in no time, he spotted dark green radish tassels. Sunlight shone through the tassels upon an expanse of red radish tops. He was about to emerge from the jute field when he quietly shrank back after seeing an old man crawling along a ridge in the radish field, taking wheat seeds from a sack and planting them one at a time in the furrows between the ridges. The autumn sun proudly shone down on his back. A light wind stirred up dust that landed on his sweat-soaked white jacket and turned it brown along the wet spots. Hei-hai crawled backwards a few metres and flattened out, resting his chin in his hands so he could see the radishes through the jute stalks. Great numbers of red eyes looked back at him from the field, and the tassels were transformed into black hair that fluttered like bird feathers.

A red-faced young man strode over from the sweet potato patch and stopped behind the old man. 'Hey!' he said abruptly. 'Did you say we had a thief last night, old man?'

The old man scrambled to his feet and stood with his hands at his sides. 'Yes,' he said, 'he stole six radishes and left the tassels behind, plus eight sweet potatoes, but he didn't take the vines.'

'Probably one of those assholes working on the flood-gate. Keep an eye out. Wait a while before coming in for lunch.'

'That's what I'll do, brigade commander,' the old man said.

Hei-hai and the old man watched the red-faced man climb the levee. The old man sat down in the radish field, directly facing a panicky Hei-hai, who backed up some more. Now the dense jute plants blocked his view.

'Hei-hai!'

'Hei-hai!'

Juzi and the mason were on the crest of the levee calling to him in the jute field. The sun was behind them, shining on workers leaving the site.

'I saw him slip into the jute,' she said. 'I think he went in to piss.'

'I wonder if the one-eyed ogre was abusing him again,' he said.

'Hei-hai!'

'Hei-hai!'

Two voices, one female, the other male, swept over the tips of jute plants like gliding swallows; the house swallows skimming after grey moths flew off in fright, and did not land for a long while. The blacksmith stood in front of the bridge opening, his good eye on the man and woman standing shoulder to shoulder; he felt his stomach begin to swell. Moments earlier, when the woman and the mason had come looking for Hei-hai, the way they talked and acted, a stranger would have thought they were looking for their own child. 'Just wait,' he fumed under his breath, 'you damned lowlifes!'

'Hei-hai! Hei-hai!' Juzi called out. 'He probably crawled into the jute field and fell asleep.'

'We should go look for him, don't you think?'

'I don't know, should we? Yes, let's do.'

They walked hand in hand into the jute field. The blacksmith ran up the levee and watched the wave-like motion of jute leaves as the stalks rustled, hearing one male and one female voice calling out 'Hei-hai', the sound seeming to come from underwater.

Tired of crawling, Hei-hai sighed and rolled over, looking up at the sun. He lay on a bed of dry sand, thinly covered with jute leaves, pillowing his head on his hands, his belly seeming to cave in; a yellow leaf with red spots floated down and covered the coal dust in his navel. He looked up at the sky and saw blue sunbeams of varying widths filtering down through the leafy canopy. The jute leaves were like a flock of golden sparrows in an aerial dance. At other times the golden sparrows seemed like moths, the spots on their wings dancing happily, like the brown film over the young blacksmith's eye.

'Hei-hai!'

'Hei-hai!'

The familiar sounds brought him out of his dream state. He sat up and bumped a thick jute stalk with his arm.

'That boy, he must be asleep.'

'I don't think so, not the way we've been calling him. He probably slipped away home.'

'The little imp . . .'

'It's really nice here . . .'

'Yes, it is . . .'

Their voices grew softer, like fish blowing bubbles on the surface. Hei-hai felt a faint electrical current pass through him and became nervous. Up on his knees, he shifted his ears and adjusted his sight until his gaze slipped past all obstructions and he saw his friends, their bodies split and sectioned by the jute stalks. A breeze set the leaves of stilled jute plants in motion, but not the stalks. A few more leaves fell to the ground, and Hei-hai heard them stir the air. He was surprised and puzzled to see a crimson bandana float down onto the jute plants, where it was caught on thorns, a silent banner. Then the red checked jacket was on the ground. The jute plants rushed toward him like surging waves. Slowly he got to his feet, turned his back, and started walking, a strange feeling crashing over him.

Chapter Five

Juzi and the mason appeared to forget about Hei-hai over the next couple of weeks, and even stopped going to the bridge to see him. At noon and night, he heard meadowlark songs in the jute field, which always brought a cold grin to his face, as if he knew what the bird was saying. The blacksmith did not notice the meadowlark's call until several days after Hei-hai. From his place under the bridge he discovered the woman and the mason's secret by careful observation. Whenever the meadowlark call sounded, the mason was absent from the worksite. The young woman, beset with anxiety, would look around before laying down her hammer and walking off. Not long after she left, the meadowlark stopped singing. Then an awful look would disfigure the blacksmith's face, and he would be spoiling for a fight. He began drinking. Hei-hai bought him a bottle of potato spirits every day from the little shop across the bridge.

On this night, waves of moonlight cascaded down like water as the meadowlark sang. A warm and tender southerly breeze wafted from the jute field to the worksite. The blacksmith grabbed a liquor bottle and downed half of it in one go, drawing tears from his good eye. Deputy Director Liu Taiyang had gone home for his son's wedding, and the workers were slacking off. Masons scheduled to work at night lay under the bridge and smoked, and with no chisels to repair, the forge fires all but died out.

'Hei-hai, go get me some radishes . . .' The alcohol burned in the blacksmith's stomach; he was nearly breathing fire.

Hei-hai stood by the bellows, stiff as a post, staring at him.

'Are you waiting for me to give you a beating?'

Hei-hai walked into the moonlight, skirted the jute field with its many mysteries, and walked through the multi-hued sweet potato field to reach the radish field, which teemed with mirages. By the time he returned with a radish, the blacksmith was snoring loudly in bed. Hei-hai laid the radish on the anvil and stirred the fire with tremulous hands, but was unable to make those blue and yellow flames dance again. He changed angles, glancing at the radish on the anvil. It seemed wrapped in a dark red cloth, tattered and ugly. He hung his head in dejection.

Hei-hai slept badly that night, tossing and turning under the bridge. Now that Director Liu was gone, all the workers went home to sleep, leaving nothing but a thin layer of straw under the bridge. Moonbeams slanted into the openings, filling them with a cold glint that was accompanied by the sounds of flowing water, rustling jute plants and the snores of the blacksmith, who slept under the westernmost arch. There were other, more puzzling sounds as well, all of which found their way into his ears. He was mesmerised by the shimmering straw spread on the stone floor, so he stacked it and burrowed in. When the wind still found its way into the pile, he curled up and stopped moving. He wanted to sleep, but sleep eluded him. He could not stop thinking about that radish. What kind was it? Golden, yet transparent. One moment he was standing in the middle of the river, and the next in the radish field. He was searching, searching everywhere.

The next morning, before the sun was up and when the moon still showed weakly in the sky, a panicky flock of crows flew over from the worksite, cawing loudly. Their dirty feathers dotted the floodgate. A dozen grey clouds stood on the eastern horizon like tall trees, tattered streamers dangling from their branches.

When he crawled out from under the bridge, Hei-hai was freezing, shivering as he had a few days earlier during an attack of the shakes. Director Liu had returned the day before, and was furious with what he found. He'd fulminated against the workers, who had showed up early on this day to work extra hard. The constant sound of hammering was like the croaking of pond frogs. There were many chisels to repair, and the blacksmith attacked them with great industry, turning out beautiful work. The masons who came to exchange the worn chisels praised his work, saying he'd surpassed the old blacksmith; the chisels tore through the rocks.

As the sun climbed into the sky, the mason came with two chisels to be repaired. Newly purchased, they were worth four or five *yuan* apiece. As the blacksmith glanced at the spirited mason, a cold ray of light shot from his good eye. The mason was unmindful of the man's expression – the eyes of the very happy only see happiness. Hei-hai knew that the blacksmith was going to try to make a fool out of the mason, and that frightened him. The blacksmith heated the two chisels until they were white as silver, laid them on the anvil and hammered the ends into points. Then he dunked them all at once in the bucket.

The mason walked off with the chisels. The grinning blacksmith eyed Hei-hai. 'What makes that asshole think he's good enough to use my chisels?' he said. 'What do you think, son?'

Hei-hai cowered in a corner. Before long, the mason returned with the chisels and flung them at the blacksmith's feet. 'One-eye,' he growled, 'what kind of work is this?'

'What are you shouting about, asshole?'

'Open that eye of yours and take a look.'

'They must be flawed chisels.'

'Bullshit! You did this to make me look bad.'

'So what if I did? Just looking at you makes my blood boil!'

'You, you . . .' The mason was white with rage. 'Come over here if you've got the balls!'

'I'm not scared of you.' The blacksmith untied his oilcloth apron, baring his back, and moved toward the mason like a brown bear.

After taking off his jacket and red athletic shirt, the mason stood on the sandy ground in front of the floodgate in his undershirt. He was tall and husky, with a student's face, solid as a tree. The blacksmith's feet, still covered with oilcloth to protect them from the hot metal, scraped noisily along the rocky ground. He had long arms, stumpy legs and a muscular chest.

'Do we talk it out or fight it out?' the blacksmith asked scornfully.

'Up to you,' the mason said in the same contemptuous tone.

'Then you'd better go home and have your father sign a guarantee that he won't come to me for a new son after I beat you to a pulp.'

'And you'd better go home to prepare your coffin.'

After a spate of insults, the two men drew closer. Hei-hai remained cowering in the corner. He watched the first exchange, which was comical. The mason spat in the blacksmith's face. Then the blacksmith swung at the mason, who stepped back, the fist missing its mark. More spit, more swings, another retreat, another miss. But before the mason could spit a third time, the blacksmith hit him on the shoulder, spinning him around.

A crowd gathered, amid startled cries. 'Stop fighting,' they shouted. 'Stop it!' But no one broke it up, and the shouts soon died out. Everyone held their breath and watched wide-eyed as the two combatants, utterly unlike in physique, pitted strength against strength. Juzi, her face white with fear, gripped the shoulders of the woman next to her. Each time her lover was hit, she moaned, the area around her eyes like dark chrysanthemums.

As they traded punch for punch, neither appeared to be winning. The mason's height served him well, but his showy punches lacked steam, and he could not put his opponent down. The blacksmith's movements were slow, but his powerful fists landed with authority, and spun the mason around. Then one of the mason's punches connected, rocking the stunned blacksmith. Seeing an opening, the mason attacked, raining punches on the blacksmith, who hunched over, stuck his head under the mason's arms and wound his arms around his waist. The mason held the blacksmith in a headlock, and they began wrestling, advancing and retreating, back and forth, ending with the mason flat on his back on the sandy ground.

Shouts erupted from the crowd.

The blacksmith stood up, spitting blood and tilting his head, like the winner at a cockfight.

The mason got up off the ground and charged. Two bodies, one light, the other dark, were once again entwined. This time the mason stayed low to protect his belly, crotch and thighs. Four arms grappled. The mason was sometimes able to pick the blacksmith up and whirl him around, but could not throw him down. He was panting heavily and sweating from head to toe; there was not a drop of sweat on the blacksmith. The mason's strength was ebbing, his movements were erratic and he was seeing double. As he slackened, the blacksmith broke his hold and wrapped his arms around the man's waist so tightly he couldn't breathe. He was back on the ground again.

The mason lost the third round badly. The blacksmith crouched down, lifted him up on his shoulders and flung him at least two metres.

Juzi, weeping, rushed over to help the mason to his feet. The pleasure vanished from the blacksmith's face as he heard her cry, replaced by a look of misery. As he stood there blankly, the mason got to his feet, pushed Juzi's hands away, scooped up a handful of sand and flung it into the blacksmith's face, temporarily blinding him. The blacksmith roared like a wild animal and frantically rubbed his good eye. The mason charged, throttling the blacksmith and forcing him to the ground, where he pummelled him as if he were beating a drum.

At that moment, a dark figure burrowed out from between the legs of the crowd. It was Hei-hai. He flew like a bird onto the back of the mason, grabbed his cheeks with hands like black claws and pulled with all his might. The man bared his teeth, parted his lips and screamed – 'Ow, ow!' – before thumping to the sandy ground again.

The blacksmith struggled to sit up and began feeling around on the ground for rocks, picking them up and flinging them in all directions. 'Bastard! Lousy dog!' Curses flew with the rocks, landing on the onlookers like a hailstorm. They scattered. Juzi screamed, and the blacksmith's hand stopped dead. Tears had washed the sand out of his eye, which could now see, though not clearly. He saw a white sliver of stone lodged in Juzi's right eye, as if she'd grown a fungus. With a screech, he covered his eye and fell to the ground, where he writhed in agony.

Hei-hai's hands relaxed the moment he heard her scream. His fingers had dug two bloody, coal-smeared gouges in the mason's cheeks. In the midst of chaos, he slinked over to a spot under the bridge and squatted down in the darkest corner he could find to watch the pandemonium at the worksite, his teeth chattering.

Chapter Six

There was no sign of the mason or Juzi the next day at the worksite, which was shrouded in gloom. Overhead the sun seemed to be convulsing, while below a bleak autumn wind raised waves in the jute field, over which flocks of sparrows cried out fearfully. The wind raised dust as it passed under the bridge and coloured much of the sky yellow. It did not die down until after nine o'clock, when the sun returned to normal.

When Deputy Director Liu Taiyang, who had returned from his son's wedding, learned what had happened, he seethed. Standing in front of the forge, he tore into the blacksmith, threatening to gouge out his good eye and give it to Juzi in exchange for the one she'd lost. The blacksmith said nothing in his defence. The pimples on his dark face had turned red. He took in big gulps of air and swallowed big gulps of alcohol.

The masons, driven by demonic energy, worked feverishly. Dull chisels piled up by the forge, waiting to be repaired. The blacksmith lay curled on his bed, swigging alcohol, the bridge opening reeking of it.

Director Liu kicked him furiously. 'Scared? Or faking it? Do you think playing dead will solve your problem? Get your ass up and repair those chisels. Maybe that will make up for what you did.'

The blacksmith flung his bottle up onto the bridge, where it shattered and rained shards of glass and drops of alcohol onto Director Liu's head. The blacksmith jumped up and ran out, listing sideways as he shouted, "What am I afraid of? The heavens don't scare me, death doesn't scare me either, so what's there to be afraid of?' He climbed up to the floodgate. 'No man scares me!' He banged into the stone railing and staggered.

'Watch out, blacksmith,' people below shouted. 'You'll fall.'

'Me, fall?' He laughed loud and hard as he climbed onto the railing. Then he let go and stood precariously. The people watching below were frozen, entranced, barely breathing.

He stretched out his arms, flapping them as if they were wings, and started walking along the narrow railing, swaying from side to side. A walk became a saunter, a saunter became a trot. Down below, the people covered their eyes with their hands, but only for a moment.

He wobbled as he ran across the railing. His distorted image was reflected on the surface of the blue water below. He ran from west to east and back, singing.

From Beijing to Nanjing I've never seen anyone
string up an electric light in their pants, tada, tada,
tadac, from Nanjing to Beijing I've never seen any-
one pull a slingshot out of their pants . . .

Some intrepid masons ran up to bring the blacksmith
down. He fought them. 'Don't fuck with me! I'm a
champion acrobat. Who's better, those girls who walk
tightropes in movies or me on this railing, tell me that.'
The masons were breathing hard by the time they got him
back down under the bridge, where he collapsed onto
his bed, foaming at the mouth. He tore at his own throat.
'Mother!' he shouted. 'I can't take it anymore. Hei-hai,
my apprentice, save your master, dig me up a radish . . .'

The sight of Hei-hai in a coat that reached his thighs
surprised the people. It was made of new heavy canvas,
durable enough to last five years or more. So little of his
shorts showed they could have been mistaken for the
hem of the coat. He was wearing a new pair of sneakers
that were too big for him, tied so tightly it looked like he
was wearing fat-headed catfish on his feet.

'Did you hear that, Hei-hai? What your master told
you to do?' said an old mason as he poked him in the
back with the stem of his pipe.

Hei-hai walked out from under the bridge, clambered up the levee and slipped into the jute field, through which a little path had been worn; plants on both sides leaned away. He walked and walked, stopping next to a spot where the plants had been flattened, as if someone had rolled over them. He rubbed his eyes with the backs of his hands, sobbed briefly, then continued on. A bit farther, he lay on the ground and crawled into the radish field. There was no sign of the skinny old man, so he stood up, walked into the middle of the field and crouched down.

Purple shoots had grown from the wheat seeds sown in the furrows. He fell to his knees and dug up a radish. There was a sound like a bubble popping as the thin roots parted from the earth. Hei-hai raptly followed the sound as it rose into the sky. There were no clouds to impede the falling rays of the bright, glorious autumn sun. He held the radish up to examine it in the sunlight, hoping to see again the strange sight he'd witnessed on the anvil that night; he wanted the sunlit radish he was holding to take on a glittering transparency and emit a golden halo, like the radish now hidden in the river. It disappointed him. It was not transparent, and it was not exquisite. It had no golden halo, much less silvery liquid inside. Again he dug up a radish and held it up to the sun, and again he was disappointed. Things were simple after that: he crawled on his knees, dug up radishes and raised them up to the sun. Tossed them away, crawled some more, dug, raised, examined, tossed.

The eyes of the old man in charge of the field were like pools of murky water. He was crouched in a cabbage patch picking caterpillars. He picked one and pinched it between his fingers, then picked another. It was nearly noon when he got to his feet to wake up the brigade commander, who was sleeping in the watchman's shed. Unable to sleep the night before, he had chosen the shed for a nap, as the village would be too noisy; the shed was perfect, with its murmur of autumn insects. The old man's vertebrae cracked as he straightened up. His attention was caught by a red nimbus over the sunlit radish field, as if it were aflame. Shading his eyes, he started walking, quickly arriving at the radish field. There he discovered that the red nimbus came from immature radishes that had been pulled out of the ground.

'Hey, you!' he bellowed, spotting the boy kneeling on the ground and holding a large radish up to the sun. His eyes, so big and bright, made the old man uneasy, but that did not stop him from grabbing the boy, jerking him to his feet and dragging him over to the watchman's shed, where he awakened the brigade commander.

'We've got a problem, brigade commander. This bear cub has dug up half our radishes.'

The sleepy man ran to the radish field to see for himself; he returned with murder in his eyes and gave

Hei-hai a swift kick. Hei-hai rose slowly, but the man slapped him while he was still dizzy.

'What village are you from, you little prick?'

Hei-hai's disoriented eyes clear as tears.

'Who sent you to sabotage us?'

Hei-hai's eyes were filled with water.

'What's your name?'

The water in Hei-hai's eyes sparkled.

'What's your father's name?'

Two lines of tears rolled down Hei-hai's face.

'Damned if he isn't a mute.'

Hei-hai's lips quivered.

'Give him a break, brigade commander, let him go.'

'Let him go?' He smiled. 'I will.'

The brigade commander stripped Hei-hai of his new coat, his new sneakers, even his shorts. He wadded them all up and tossed them into a corner. 'Go home and tell your father to come claim your clothes. Now get out of here!'

Hei-hai turned to leave. At first he shyly covered his privates with his hands, but dropped them after a few steps. The old man sobbed at the sight of the dirty, naked boy.

Hei-hai slipped into the jute field like a fish that has swum into the ocean. The jute leaves rustled under the shimmering autumn sun.

'Hei-hai!'

'Hei-hai!'

PENGUIN
SPECIALS

Marrow
YAN LIANKE

Translated from the original Chinese by Carlos Rojas

In a small village deep in the Balou Mountains, Fourth Wife You despairs of what the future holds for her four mentally-impaired children. A cure for the family curse appears, but it will extract a price so primal and complete that no one can be expected to make it except, perhaps, for a mother. A chilling and relentless tale of family responsibility and a mother's sacrifice, *Marrow* is Yan Lianke at his best.

Yan Lianke was born in 1958 in Henan Province, China. He has been called a 'master of imaginative satire' by the *New York Times*. His writing oscillates between military themes and the Chinese countryside, the absurdly dark descriptions of which lend a surrealist setting to his works. He is the author of *Serve the People!*, *Lenin's Kisses*, *Dream of Ding Village* and *The Four Books*, and the recipient of the 2014 Franz Kafka Prize.

'We authors live for the sake of our memories and feelings, and it is therefore these memories and feelings that transform us into writers.'
– *Yan Lianke*